ONCE UPON A TIME IN
India

BETHANY BELLEMIN

Copyright © 2023 Bethany Bellemin.

All rights reserved. No part of this book may be reproduced, stored, or transmitted by any means—whether auditory, graphic, mechanical, or electronic—without written permission of both publisher and author, except in the case of brief excerpts used in critical articles and reviews. Unauthorized reproduction of any part of this work is illegal and is punishable by law.

ISBN: 979-8-89031-834-3 (sc)
ISBN: 979-8-89031-835-0 (hc)
ISBN: 979-8-89031-836-7 (e)

Because of the dynamic nature of the Internet, any web addresses or links contained in this book may have changed since publication and may no longer be valid. The views expressed in this work are solely those of the author and do not necessarily reflect the views of the publisher, and the publisher hereby disclaims any responsibility for them.

One Galleria Blvd., Suite 1900, Metairie, LA 70001
(504) 702-6708

Contents

Chapter 1   It Begins 1

Chapter 2   Arrival in India 7

Chapter 3   Life Like the Raj 15

Chapter 4   Explanations 25

Chapter 5   The Hunt Begins in Earnest 35

Chapter 6   Change of Pace 43

Chapter 7   Patrick's Help 51

Chapter 8   Deeper Thinking 61

Chapter 9   Final Steps 71

Chapter 10   From Beginning to End 77

Epilogue 87

Facts or Fiction? 89

From the Author 91

CHAPTER 1

It Begins

The year was 1860 when it all began. Up to that year, I had been a shy lad, short for my age, but considered rather clever, at least at school. My scores had been high, and my classmates rather resented me for it. I had few friends, but then I never really had friends at any time. At least before 1860. Good grades weren't enough. It was never enough.

My grandmother raised me with an iron hand, yet with pride. She was proud of me in her way, and I knew this and was comforted to know it. But her money was dwindling, having raised two sons, one dying in the war and the other vanishing to India some years before I was born. Funds were outgoing, but not incoming. As the proverb says, "Riches take wings" and the money in that house was simply racing away.

My father, the elder of her sons, had died in the service of the Royal Navy. My mother was a gentle creature.

"Weak," as my grandmother would say with a sniff of disdain. My mother soon followed my father to the grave, and I was orphaned at eight years of age.

My grandmother gave me good care; sharp clothes, the best of schools, and after all my expenses, combined with the vast fortune she paid in searching for her lost son, her fortune was nearly spent. After the holiday season of 1859, I was pulled from school, and though I was now fourteen, I looked younger, and it made my grandmother uneasy. She feared I might become sickly like my mother, but I soon found out that my grandmother's health was failing as fast as the bank funds.

In February, she received a package that made her quite livid. For some days I heard her muttering furiously to herself and she hardly spoke a word to me, only keeping Tennyson, her long-employed and very faithful butler, in her confidence. Aside from Tennyson, there was a cheaply kept cook whose former position had been at a tenement house; the house was otherwise bare of servants by this time. I was quite alone during these days and kept out of sight though within call of my grandmother.

For a week she roamed about in this distressed state before she abruptly took to her room. A doctor was called in, but after an unfavorable report, my grandmother threw a vase at him and demanded he leave the premises immediately.

"I knew that before you came, you pompous, bloodsucking fool!" she shouted. I was quite jarred at this for I had been shamefully eavesdropping. The doctor left in a huff and Tennyson paid him at the door. Tennyson, the well-trained butler that he was, stoically cleaned up the fragments of the vase. But I finally knew the awful truth; my grandmother had a bad heart, and we were nearly bankrupt.

The next day was a dismal rainy day when Tennyson called me upstairs.

"Master James, it's time, you know. She's been a hard woman I'll allow, but she loves you in her fashion. You remind her much of her own son, the one she lost to India. But now you see there's something that's, well been a bit of a shock. I, er, that is—"

"Tennyson, stop babbling!" my grandmother shouted from her room. "Tell him at once or let me tell and be done with it!"

Tennyson smiled, "Remarkable hearing she has, eh?" He ushered me into the room and bowed to leave, but she stopped him.

"No, stay, it's nothing you don't already know." She turned to me with that deep frown and for a moment it seemed most unlikely that she had a bad heart, for she appeared as powerful as ever.

"James, it's no use beating about the bush, there's no money, well hardly any, and my days are getting short. I married your grandfather at age twenty. I had some social standing back then, but I have had the misfortune to outlive all my relatives, as well as acquaintances. There's no one left to help you here. In England that is. Your uncle, Robert," her voice shook a bit, and I realized it was the first time I had heard her say his name.

"Robert left for adventure when he was young. The last anyone knew of him was that he had been seen in Calcutta. Well, he hasn't been seen since, and those detectives I've been paying grew quite fat on their salary. For I now know he went to settle in a jungle province and raised an estate. He married but had no children. He sent me several letters which quite suspiciously never made it out of India until now. I've read over them, thirty-seven in all. He died and so did his wife. He never heard that your father had died before and left the estate to him. So that makes *you* his heir and now it is yours."

She was exhausted at this point and paused for a drink of water. "How did he die?" I asked timidly.

"Oh, some heathen disease, something about the heat and bugs. His lawyer has a note he sent explaining it all with his will. His wife, your aunt, was some sort of Indian princess it seems, but no one is disputing his family's claim to his inheritance. At least you'll have something. But there is a very peculiar demand. He left it in his will. You must live at the estate for one year and find the "*lost piece*" before you can claim the bulk of the fortune. Ridiculous, but Robert did have his games, so you'll have to play. And really, James, you're a smart lad, rather like your grandfather if I may be so bold as to brag. You'll work it out alright. You can't legally become full proprietor until you turn eighteen, of course, laws and all that, but the lawyer can act as your estate manager until then. And you know Robert has been dead for nearly a year; time is getting short for you to claim it. I suppose you ought to leave within a fortnight or sooner if it can be arranged. Tennyson will see to it." Then she waved me away. And that was all.

For several days Tennyson went over train and boat travel with me, while I packed. I felt quite wrong about leaving my grandmother in this state and said so.

"Well, I certainly don't want you waiting about while I die!" was her snappish response. But I understood she did not want me to witness her strength fail. She wished to be remembered as the strong one. So, I bid her goodbye and left. I knew I wouldn't see her again.

The trip was long, but I spent most of it reading my uncle's numerous letters and studying up on India. By the time the last boat stopped at the last port, I was as prepared as I could be.

CHAPTER 2

Arrival in India

I disembarked in Calcutta and found I had a two-hour wait for my train to depart. After seeing to my luggage and asking directions from the conductor, I found a small cookery (with affordable food). My funds were getting very low by this time.

It was a short time later that I emerged into the hot crowded street again and prepared to wait the rest of the time at the train station. But it was at this time a twist happened which caused a definite change in my affairs. A street boy bumped into me, and I was slow to realize that he had stolen my wallet. I was soon chasing after him, though the crowd apprehended my progress. I was extremely fortunate at this time to leap up on top of a barrel and catch sight of him pelting down an alley.

As foolish as it was, I followed, quite desperate to retrieve my wallet. The alley dead-ended at a wall and there sat the boy smugly counting out my money. Upon seeing me, he drew a knife and, for lack of prudence on my part, I dove at him.

I confess that having been bullied at school I could when in a temper box quite well. And I was in a hot temper now. The boy cut me twice, though not badly, but it angered me even more and I pummeled him to the ground.

"Quarter!" he shouted after his knife was knocked from his hand. I drew back and we stared panting at each other. He threw the wallet at me with a snarl, and I snatched it up. Now that my temper had cooled, I was aware that the boy was only half Indian and by his voice was also unmistakably British.

"What are you staring at!" he snapped. I shook my head.

"I think I'm looking at a waste of talent!" And then, as so often happens after a good muddle, we both began to laugh. We shook hands and he said his name was Patrick, but the street vendors called him the "street rajah." It was a mean name; he was half proud, half ashamed of it.

"I could get you a bite to eat," I offered by way of apology for the whopping black eye he would soon be sporting. He shook his head in a surly way.

"A gent can't be seen with me. I'm a half-crown shame."

Arrival in India

I was a little startled at his story but suffice it to say a very dishonorable British soldier had a child by a poor Hindu woman then abandoned her. Patrick had been taken to an orphanage run by foreign money. It explained his very British-sounding English accent. The education had been rigorous, but once he was old enough to realize there was no future for him, he had planned his escape, saying that the British orphanage had given no love and even less food. He had run away eventually, finding the brutality of the streets preferable. He told of avoiding the child slaves, stealing food and clothes, and pulling hijinks on the marketplace vendors. My life had been sheltered. I was shocked and humbled by these tales and I felt very rich compared to poor Patrick.

By this time, I realized my train would be leaving shortly and, in a panic, asked how to get to the depot. Patrick led me himself and by the time we arrived we were fast friends.

"I've got enough left to buy you a ticket to come with me. Do come, Patrick. I don't know anyone else in India."

But no persuading would get him to comply. In the end, he promised that if he could get the money on his own, he would come up to Kasauli where my uncle's house was. I did admonish him to at least not steal the funds to which he winked and handed me my watch which I had not even realized was missing. The train whistle blew, and we parted.

It seemed ages later, though only a few days when I reached Kasauli. My journey had ranged from boat to train to cart and finally I was close. I had to ask for directions to the *Jokhim House Manor*, my uncle's home. No one would speak to me and after wandering about, I saw a true British law office. It was only a house, but the sign hanging outside said office and I barreled inside.

I ran right into a tall, thin man with his hat on as he was just leaving.

"I say, old chap, is the town burning?" then he laughed. I picked myself up and stammered an apology. He smiled; I liked his smile even less than his laugh.

"You don't quite belong around here, no tan from the sun, and your clothes are woolen." His eye was quick, and I acknowledged I was a stranger looking for my uncle's house. His manner became slightly stiffer.

"Oh, ah then you must be James B. Harris III. You're rather earlier than anticipated."

He introduced himself, it was the very lawyer who had sent the letters and the will to my grandmother. George Gray, that was his name, offered to take me himself. A cart was procured, and I was rather alarmed to see Mr. Gray bring a pistol.

"It's not quite safe on the roads you know."

Arrival in India

We did see a rough group of fellows just outside of town, but they, after a good glaring, faded into the jungle. At last, we were coming through the gate and there it was, Jokhim Manor.

We unloaded my three bags and a young Hindu man, clad in all white with a turban and a gold chain, emerged from the house. He inclined his head respectfully to us and was introduced as Aadi, head man of the house.

Upon hearing who I was, he bowed and said a prayer in Hindi. Mr. Gray told me it was a blessing prayer for the new master of the house. I nodded my thanks, and we went into the massive dwelling. It was eerily silent inside and Mr. Gray told me only four servants had been retained since my uncle's death.

By this time, I was so tired from weeks of travel that I hardly heard the rest of the information Mr. Gray felt obliged to share. But my ears perked up as he was leaving.

"Do have a good night, old fellow. I'll be back in a day or so to explain everything to you. But be careful, I suppose that you know that Jokhim is an old house, with strange myths hovering over it. It's not called 'House of Risk' for nothing, you know. Well, cheerio!"

And he was gone. It was now dusk and only a few torches burned to brighten that dark house. Aadi showed me to a grand courtyard where three other servants stood to greet me. All promptly bowed, which I had expected, but the head housekeeper, Lipika, started wailing, which I had not expected.

I looked at Aadi who shrugged, "She laments that the curse of this household should fall on one so young."

This certainly did not raise my spirits and I requested to be shown my rooms for the night. I felt I might simply turn and run from this nightmare if I had to hear that woman's wailing echoing through the empty rooms for another second.

I was shown to what had been my uncle's chambers on the second floor. I walked in, shook my head, and walked out. Too many doors.

"Aadi," I said in the lordliest tone I could muster. "These rooms shall not do at all, wasted space. Take me to a smaller, more practical room."

The head man raised his eyebrows, only slightly, but I noticed, and led me to a smaller guest room.

It had fine windows looking east, a four-postered bed draped in mosquito netting, and a bookshelf holding a few moth-eaten bibliographies. But to my relief, this room had only one door, not several, which I could bolt from the inside.

"This will do," I stated tossing my hat to one of the bed posts. Aadi bowed and disappeared, returning three times to bring my luggage and a small dinner plate, as well as a pitcher of water to wash with.

I dismissed him with a gracious and commanding manner that could be procured from my lilting tenor voice. Alone at last, I quietly bolted the door and checked the windows. No trellis or tree was too near the window, and heavy shutters could be closed and barred. I locked myself in tight and lit every candle in my sanctuary. I felt somewhat safe, but it was nearing midnight when I finally drifted off to sleep with strange jungle sounds ringing in my ears. I had prayed every prayer I knew and fervently wished that Patrick had come with me. When I did finally sleep, it was to have restless dreams in which I had lost something and could not find it: my courage.

CHAPTER 3

Life Like the Raj

The next morning, I woke to hear Aadi knocking on the door.

"*Malika*," which I soon found out meant, employer or boss, "Will you have the morning meal in your quarters or on the veranda?" I rose up and stared at my odd surroundings. I knew today would be crucial if I were to survive in this house. I had to convey that I was confident, content to be here, and owner of this inheritance.

"The veranda will do. Thank you, Aadi." I heard him walk away then I pounced out of bed to open my blockade defenses. I was determined that no one would see me as a coward. I flung the shutters back and gasped. A glorious garden, kissed with sunshine shone green and shady below me. Exotic birds flew about squawking and twittering, while vibrant flowers spilled their perfume into the air. A langur monkey was busy stealing fruit from the trees, and in the distance, outside the compound, an elephant trumpeted. It was the kind of scene that stirs the heart, and my somewhat unimaginative mind felt an awakening that made me tingle from head to foot. I dressed hurriedly and went downstairs, though I did get rather confused in one of the corridors. But finally, I was in the courtyard, and beyond the broad doors was the veranda, where the smell of food alerted me to my extreme hunger.

Aadi waited on me while I ate, and Lipika presented herself to ask if I had any changes to make for the housekeeping. I couldn't think of an answer, but I thanked her for the cleanliness and said I would tour the house first before giving my orders. I felt it was a grand excuse for thoroughly exploring that vast house without being disturbed. It worked capitally well for after breakfast the servants vanished, and I began my exploration. I won't bore you with the immense details that filled every room, but I will describe the one room that intrigued me the most.

It was the study, filled with books, oriental rugs, valuable tapestries, and a large wooden desk. The desk was quite solid, for when I tried to push it against a bookshelf so I could browse through the volumes on the upper shelves, I couldn't budge the ponderous item. I contented myself with flipping through the more accessible books. I had missed books since quitting school and felt a certain sense of peace to be holding the words of wiser men than I once again.

My uncle had been a man of taste and clearly had housed a thirst for knowledge. His library ranged from Shakespeare to Aristotle.

I sat down on the desk and glanced around wondering why there was no chair. And now that I had a moment to think, I realized several pieces of furniture seemed to be arranged oddly and even missing throughout the house. It was too many pieces to be a mere mistake in my uncle's furniture arrangements. I determined to ask Lipika about it. I stopped to admire a gun collection, and though most of the firearms were fine works of craftsmanship, all were rusting and in need of cleaning. I decided I would tend to that task myself over the course of my stay.

At the lunch hour, I came into the kitchen to find Ida (Lipika's assistant), Yatin the chef, Lipika herself, and Aadi all whispering amongst themselves. As I walked in, their voices ceased and I followed their gaze to the window. A tattered shawl was hanging on a tree branch in the courtyard.

"It's a sign. It belonged to the old master's wife. She must be angry with the newcomer," Lipika said aloud, very shrilly. That woman was always nearing hysterics. I did not speak but went outside and jerked it down only to find that same langur, fruit-stealing monkey from earlier was holding tightly to the other end. It screamed and yanked like a spoiled child, but I wrested the torn cloth away. "Bad monkey," I said sharply to which it ran higher up the tree and pouted. It occurred to me he might have been a pet of my aunt and uncle. Upon reentering the house, I asked Aadi about it. The monkey had been a pet, *her* pet, my aunt's own personal darling.

"I suppose he misses her and stole this garment away since it had been hers," was my practical explanation.

The servants seemed only slightly convinced and I demanded possession of all the keys. I didn't want any more loose clothing lying about to scare me out of my wits. I proceeded to lock all the wardrobes, one of which was open, and I saw the monkey peering in at the window.

I felt sorry for the creature in spite of myself. Approaching the window, I offered him a little gold elephant statue.

"Here's a plaything if you want something to play with, but for heaven's sake, don't go on scaring everyone."

The monkey sidled forward then abruptly snatched the statue away and shrieked at me. I shrugged; it wouldn't do to take offense from a monkey's temper.

I was tired of that house by this time and decided to explore the gardens. Outside was beautiful and even more so after going through the dim corridors. I meandered around fountains, fruit trees, and luxurious beds of rich green grass until I found myself at an ornately carved iron gate. I tried my keys and found one turned the rusting bolt. Opening it, I found myself in a jungle that was rapidly reclaiming the walkways. It certainly would be unsafe to venture any distance into the jungle alone and unarmed. I hesitated, then saw ahead of me in a tree sat that langur monkey. He chirruped to me in a funny way, and I almost unconsciously walked the path toward him. He went a little farther ahead and then clambered down to the ground. He edged into the brush and squealed. I stepped into a little jungle alcove, dark and green, with vines drooping down like curtains.

Two large irregular stones stood solemnly in that little sanctuary, and, on a hunch, I scraped away the moss and growth. They were tombstones. One was marked Robert Bryan Harris. 1820 to 1858. An odd inscription followed.

"Link by link, and yard by yard."[1] It was a direct reference to Charles Dickens's still rather avant-garde story written seventeen years before. It was strange to me I had not seen this

---

[1] Dickens, Charles, *A Christmas Carol*, England, originally printed by Chapman & Hall, 1843, reprinted by Miller, Son and Co. 1922, page 30.

book in the library. And perhaps this was part of the "missing piece" he had referred to in his will. Was it the answer or another clue?

One thing I knew, no one had been by these tombs for quite some time. Except for the monkey. I noticed that he seemed to be drooping like the place made him remember what he had lost. The other stone said, "Kashvi, my beloved wife. Buried after her culture's fashion and beliefs. This place marks no grave, only memory." Somehow, this disturbed me more than if it had been her actual grave. An empty grave seemed a bit ominous. I plucked a few wildflowers from nearby vines and laid them at the foot of the tombstones. I bowed my head respectfully for a moment then went back to the path. As I left, I glanced back and saw the monkey looking very forlorn.

"You coming?" I asked. The monkey cautiously followed me back to the gate. Once back in the garden, the creature gave me a long stare before scrambling back into the trees. I had the queer feeling that the monkey knew quite a few things that had me muddled concerning this entire situation.

I marched inside and found Aadi. "Why is my uncle's grave in such a disrespectful state?"

He looked uncomfortable and after stammering "*Sahib*" a few times, he cleared his throat and murmured, "Here in my country, we tend to our dead differently from your country. As your uncle was not my religion, I respect his memory in different ways."

Out of respect for his beliefs, I let the matter drop and turned the conversation. "Can you give a reason for the missing furniture?"

He glanced around and said very softly, "Sahib, this is a strange house, things have happened that I cannot explain. Since your uncle died, I have found furniture rearranged and small pieces, chairs mostly, have disappeared."

I gave Aadi a long stare. He was not lying, but he also was not a man to be easily frightened.

"I do not believe in ghosts, Aadi."

Aadi stood to his full height, "Sahib, I was educated abroad at the expense of my former *Svami*, your uncle. My religious side believes in things unseen; my educated side knows there is logic in most events. But things have happened since his death that cannot be understood."

"Well spoken," I ascended. Somehow, I felt Aadi would be someone I could trust with anything.

"Aadi, I want all the locks checked daily for signs of tampering. I also have a boy in Calcutta I would like found and brought here. He is called Patrick, and sometimes known as the street rajah. Please arrange a man to be hired to find him."

I gave him my watch, "He'll know this." I also gave him money to attend to the matter. "And please send for him quickly."

"I will go myself. It will arouse less talk in the village." He bowed and left immediately. I felt a wave of relief and understood the special relationship between my grandmother and Tennyson. Having someone you could depend on in the house was a true treasure. And suddenly I realized my duty as "Lord of the Manor." My servants should be trusted companions and should know I was a good employer, fair, and just. I resolved I would be such a man and went into the library to plan how I would handle the near future. I made a list of what I knew about my uncle and on a separate page wrote down all of the "clues" I had at this point. There was something my uncle had hidden, and his clues would have led my father, the assumed to be heir, to this item.

I was not my father and had never known my uncle. My disadvantages in this regard were certainly hampering my progress. But I was keenly aware that someone was looking for the "missing piece." Someone was stealing furniture, moving items, and (intentionally or not), certainly scaring the servants in this respect. My list of suspects was short, and to be honest I felt that the servants were not involved in any way whatsoever.

I now knew that my aunt had died before my uncle as indicated by her epitaph. I carefully copied down the words written on both tombstones. At the very least, they held a key to what my uncle was leading me to.

Now "piece" I knew could refer to a gun, often referred to as a hunter's piece. It could refer to a piece of furniture which had obviously occurred to another unknown individual. It could be a piece of jewelry, this might explain the Dickens quote "Link by link, and yard by yard."

Still, it felt like something was quite out of place. My aunt's tombstone did not seem to reference the mystery, but I pondered it as well. I thumbed through my ring of keys, but all had fit a lock that had been accounted for by myself. Once again, I perused through the horde of books looking for *A Christmas Carol*. I even fetched an ottoman and stacked it precariously on top of a stool to enable me to reach the upper shelves. My search was fruitless.

By this time, it was late evening and Lipika had long since lit the candles and torches about. Feeling frustrated, I did not eat the evening meal and proceeded to my room. Despite my unbounded curiosity and still unfamiliar surroundings, I slept soundly with the jungle noises already feeling normal.

CHAPTER 4

Explanations

The following day, I began going through all of my uncle's personal papers, ledgers, and accounts. After several hours, the only thing I discovered was that my uncle had been a wealthy man. A very wealthy man. That afternoon, the lawyer, George Gray, dropped by as he had promised.

Despite his oily manner, he was efficient at explaining everything to me. Of course, the sum of all the inheritance ended with the requirement; enough money for one year and the rest to follow only if I found the "missing piece."

Finally, when the conversation lulled over the dinner table I asked, "Tell me about my uncle. Why did none of his letters ever reach England?"

Mr. Gray lit a cigar as he pushed away from the table. My nose wrinkled at the repulsive smell, and I noticed Ida cough from her post by the door.

"Well, perhaps he never mailed them. And he did not know his brother had a son or had died so many years before. I don't suppose he would have left such complicated directions for a young fellow." His tone was dreadfully patronizing. Even Lipika put on a bit of an air as she served him, and paid extreme attention to me adding many "Sahibs" as if reminding Mr. Gray that he was a guest in my house. I felt very grateful to the housekeeper and smiled at her warmly as she poured my coffee. Another thing I had to adjust to in India: coffee.

Mr. Gray preferred something stronger and when Lipika left to bring in a refreshment he requested, he leaned forward saying quietly, "I can't say for certain, but perhaps it was that your uncle did not wish to be found? You see, this house belonged to a great rajah many decades ago. It was built for his favorite wife, but she died young, and this house was abandoned to the jungle for quite some time. Your uncle had very little wealth until he mysteriously acquired a fortune while out on some adventure. Soon after he married her ladyship Kashvi, a daughter of fine Indian lineage, let me tell you. He reclaimed this house from the jungle and set up his manor

Explanations

estate. But many of the villagers say this house is cursed and that he disturbed the "ghosts" by moving in. It's said that he and his wife were justly killed by the curse. The servants fled except oddly enough the four you have here now. I find that highly suspicious, old chap, and I would watch them closely, especially that Aadi fellow. I say, where is Aadi? Haven't seen him all day."

"He's on an errand for me," I replied coolly. Mr. Gray knit his brows together and puffed hard on his cigar, evidently displeased at being in the dark to his whereabouts. I heard Ida cough again, and I remarked drily that perhaps he should put out his cigar. He was not pleased, but he did discard the offensive item.

When my guest finally left, his parting remark was rather sharp. "You should consult me, you know, about managing the house, after all, I am the executor of the estate until the year is up."

"Oh, I can manage quite well, thank you."

He frowned but tried to hide it with a laugh that failed miserably. "Do keep an eye on your servants, educated servants can be especially dangerous," he called over his shoulder.

To say I was completely sick of visitors after this event would properly sum up my feelings at this time.

You can imagine my chagrin when the next morning as I walked through the gardens a horseman came through the gate. He was middle-aged and rode exceptionally well. I was in no mood for guests, but one could not help admiring such equestrian finesse. He dismounted before me and introduced himself.

"Colonel Edward Baker, retired doctor of the Army. I must apologize for not coming to greet you earlier, but I was attending to a medical emergency out in a distance village."

"Pleasure to meet you, Colonel. I'm James Harris, the nephew of Robert Harris. I hope the medical emergency ended well?"

"Oh, yes, capitally, twins to be sure. Mother and children are quite healthy now."

He gave my hand a hearty shake and turning slipped a cane out of a loop on his saddle. "Mind if I take a turn about the grounds with you?"

"No, sir, please be my guest. Should I have your horse tended to?"

"No, I came at a slow walk, just stretching his legs. Old Napoleon." Here he patted the horse's glossy neck, "He is jungle-born and bred. Exceptionally well-mannered creature. He'll follow along behind us. Rather like a great dog than a horse sometimes," he chuckled and the horse nudged him affectionally. I couldn't help but like the colonel. His good humor and straightforward manner was such a relief compared to Mr. Gray's company. We walked about chatting, he treated me as quite his equal and told me helpful information about maintaining a life in India. Eventually, the conversation turned to my uncle.

"It's quite true he got his fortune most unexpectedly and I rather have my ideas where he got it. But he and Kashvi, pardon me, my time in the jungle has worsened my manners a bit, got into the habit of calling people by their Christian names. Do you mind?" I assured him I didn't mind at all. He continued his narrative, "Like I was saying, they were very happy. Kashvi had been the child of a Rajah's third wife; she really had no future until your uncle saw her at a festival. It was a fateful moment. Your uncle married and swept her to his grand place. But you know it's rather like history repeated itself. They were married for six years, and she was very much in love with Robert, I dare say she was almost passionately jealous of him. I only speak from having known her, and I did love them both as my own children. But I do think Kashvi stole and hid all of Robert's letters once he put them to be posted. After his death, Aadi found them, all tucked away in an embroidered pillow. She truly feared his family would disapprove of the marriage and I suspect she thought she could keep them away from her Robert. I am merely speculating, but she was, as I said, a jealous woman. Well, as you know, she died very young. It was consumption, and I'm afraid it settled in her lungs. She passed away within a few weeks. I treated her to my best abilities. I did beg Robert to send her to the mountains, but you see he was distraught and slow to act and then it was too late," the colonel shook his head. "And then, Robert's malaria came back with a vengeance. He barely fought through this time and became a shadow of the man I had known. He kept to himself that last year and seemed to be very concerned about something in particular, though he never did confide it to me."

We walked in silence for a moment. I listened to Napoleon's heavy hooves and bridle jangling, and the firm step of the colonel. Finally, I worked up my nerves and blurted out, "How did my uncle become so wealthy? You said you have an idea on the subject. And what is wrong with this house, what's this curse some have warned me of?"

"Well, both questions are linked together. I believe, though I have no proof of this, mind you. Robert had gone on a journey when he was younger. He said he always would get into a 'fit' to go exploring. He and two others journeyed from England to the Hindu Kush Mountains. Three years later, he came here alone and with a partly healed gunshot wound. That's when I first met him, spring of 1852. He told me of his travels, how his companions had died, knocked off one by one and he alone escaped with his shoulder wound. I asked who had killed his party, and well, I'm just saying what he told me. Though do take into account he had a dreadful fever at this time, he said 'I have found the forbidden and took it. And my friends have died for it.' But once he was fully recovered, he seemed anxious to be out again. I was quite surprised when he settled on the ruined mansion nearby. Then he would have moments of melancholy, but soon would be himself again. This house was built quite grand once upon an age and Robert restored it magnificently. But the former owner had only presided over this house for a few short years. She died in childbirth as did the baby. I suppose that Kashvi dying so young felt like a repeat of the ancient past. At least that's what so many villagers rumored about. It's said to be cursed, and whoever lives here has a miserable time ahead of them. Now, James, you mark what I say here, I do not believe in superstitions. But I have learned to respect the people that believe them. India is a strange and wonderful place, and I have grown to love it. It is odd perhaps to you as it is to so many others from the homeland, but these people are more like my fellow country folks than the country wherein I was born. There is a deep knowledge of herbs and histories and proverbs, it is rich to overflowing in these qualities. If you can, and I expect this will unhinge me to you, see them as equals, not subjects. I have become very like-minded to them in many ways, and they've gone so far in accepting me that I am allowed to doctor the sick instead of them dying of simple, curable jungle diseases. It's fulfilling, man, I tell you—fulfilling!"

He smiled broadly and called Napoleon over. As he mounted, he added, "Ask Aadi or Ida even about the treasure mines of lapis lazuli in the Hindu Kush Mountains. And I believe you will see the plausibility in believing that your uncle struck a rich vein in a mine and that is the vastness of his wealth explained." With a wave, he clicked to his mount and cantered out the gate.

I wasn't quite able to soak in all he had said and it took a few more turns around the garden to come to an understanding of it. One thing I did know is I wanted to grow to be a man as worthy of respect as the colonel. The monkey followed me about in the trees overhead chittering.

"And yet," I said aloud, "what was meant by finding the forbidden?" In response, the monkey squealed and shook the branches of his perch. I went back into the house and called for Ida. Upon being asked about the Kush Mountains, she

EXPLANATIONS

explained the endless quantities of famed emerald and lapis lazuli mined there. "And also, there is other great wealth, Sahib, the lost treasure of Nader Shah."

CHAPTER 5

The Hunt Begins in Earnest

"What lost treasure?" I asked bewildered. Ida told me of the Persian raid over a hundred years before. She told of the military leader Nader Shah who had stolen so much treasure from Delhi. His caravan hauling the loot was rumored to be 150 miles long. The legend stated that Nader was eventually murdered and later the mass of the treasure was hidden in the endless, mapless tunnels of the Hindu Kush Mountains. I learned of Nader's murderer, Adel Shah, and that much of the treasure he hid, had been lost to the mountain's secrets forever.

"It is somewhere in the darkness that the cursed treasure hides. Away from the greed of men. Let us hope the death of so many for the conquest was enough and that the riches are lost never to be found." Her voice was hushed and her eyes wide. She firmly believed in the curse of this treasure. An idea was swiftly forming into an explanation in my mind. I thanked Ida who smiled bashfully and went out of the room.

I went back to my uncle's papers with zeal and searched endlessly for more than a week and at last there it was, a document showing a mine owned in Robert Harris's name. It stated that in two years following 1849, vast tonnage of purest lapis lazuli had been mined. This would have made my uncle rich indeed. And yet the third year was unmentioned which showed my uncle's life was unknown during the space of the winter of 1851 to spring of 1852 when he met Colonel Baker. What had happened? Had he found some of this 'cursed' treasure? Is that what he had meant by saying he had taken the forbidden?

But then if he had become so very wealthy from the mine, why had he taken things from a lost treasure, and why had he told no one of it? I began to suspect that perhaps my uncle had been the greedy type, and yet such a dire characteristic did not fit into the colonel's high opinion of him. Something was certainly not clear in these events and for days I pondered on it. But I made no progress.

It had now been twenty-five days since Aadi left to find Patrick and I missed his presence, eagerly looking forward to having both of them with me. It was a bit of a shock to realize they were true friends, to me who had never had someone to call friend. This pleasant discovery made me miss them all the more, but it felt good to really miss someone. I often thought of my grandmother at this time and wondered if she thought of me, and somehow, I knew that she did, and this reassuring thought energized me to complete the searching.

I had been in the house for a month with no further progress. I was annoyed with myself and was pacing about the house deep in thought. I came into the great hall as Lipika was lighting the candles. I had been so busy with the puzzle I had not realized how late in the day it was.

"Sahib will be in here for some time?" Lipika asked with her customary bow. "Yes, this seems like a good room to think."

"Should I light the chandelier?"

I started to say no but when I looked up, my eyes widened. The chandelier was enormous and intricately designed with gold leaves. A heavy chain held it firmly aloft. And the chains were made of links!

"Lipika!" I exclaimed. "Light every available candle in this room!"

I raced past her, and though she was quite surprised at me, she dutifully began lighting the dozens of candles. I finally found a ladder after rummaging and hauled the ponderous item back to the great hall.

By this time, Ida had come tiptoeing in to see what the excitement was about. I set the ladder beside the chandelier and raced up to the top rung.

"Link by link!" I shouted as I worked my hand up the chain. And there handing on the highest link was a tiny pouch of leather, impossible to see from the ground twenty feet below. I untied the cord and brought the pouch down. Ida and Lipika watched fascinated as I opened the pouch and pulled out a small iron key—the key to hopefully unlock this mystery. Of course, I could not imagine what lock it would fit, it was an exceptionally small and plain key. Lipika and Ida glanced at each other and then back to the key.

"I have never seen that key, Sahib, but I do know the former Malika wore a leather strap at times about his neck. Perhaps he was keeping this key always on his person." Lipika spoke reverently of my uncle, the former master of Jokhim.

With these strange thoughts and circumstances in my head that night, I slept fitfully after lying awake and staring at the moon beams draping through the window onto my bedcovers. I had long since ceased to lock myself up at night. I felt safe now and at ease in this room.

The Hunt Begins in Earnest

When morning came, I came to the muddled decision that since "link by link" had been solved, then the next clue was "yard by yard." Well, could it be *yard* as in measurement or literally *yard* as in the surrounding gardens? Or perhaps it referred to something at sea, such as a yard arm, but I dismissed this last part. I had come to the conclusion that my uncle had not bought this property on a whim. He had a very specific reason. The monkey squealed from outside, and looking out the window I laughed as I answered him, "No, I do not think you were the reason he chose this house." The monkey swung about then stopped for a moment to swipe another piece of fruit from the tree. I went down to breakfast to find a telegram. Lipika was nervous that it bore bad news. But upon reading it, my face lit into a smile and she smiled as well to see the joy in my response.

It read, "Found. Returning with me." It was signed by Aadi.

"Aadi is coming home with a friend of mine."

"Very good, Sahib. I will prepare the room next to your own for the guest."

To while away the time, I spent several days scouring through the library again. I had an enjoyable time with the foreign language encyclopedias my uncle had collected. He had heavily studied languages of the Middle East judging by the numerous markings in the margins. There was a section in the stories of ancient Persia and my uncle had underlined extensively through these chapters. He certainly had been a man of many interests and pastimes. It made solving this puzzle much harder than expected. My uncle had been an enigma himself and he certainly left behind a strange trail to follow.

When Sunday came, I attended the local church, built seven years previously by the locally prominent families. I was introduced to several families and could sense the local's high level of curiosity associated with my family name. No one seemed to have been familiar with my uncle; he appeared to have been a bit of a hermit. I retreated as soon as politeness allowed me back to my house.

I spent the rest of the afternoon in the library thinking long and hard on that key from the chandelier, but no inspirations came to me. At last, in the midst of my puzzlings, a loud shout echoed from outside the house, and racing to the window, I saw Aadi riding in a cart and Patrick with him. Patrick was standing and shouting and waving all at once. I waved from the window and raced outside. Patrick and I collided on the terrace and we both talked all at once.

Aadi had outfitted him like a true Hindu lord complete with a jewel on his turban. He certainly looked the part of a prince as he stood smiling under the cool veranda roof with his one gem scattering light fragments on the mosaic tile. I

The Hunt Begins in Earnest

noticed too that his vocabulary and pronunciation of English had improved since our first meeting, and I knew Aadi had not idled time on the trip home. Already Patrick's overall speech and mannerisms reflected a new beginning in his education. I determined I would learn to speak the dialects of Hindi as well as he spoke English.

I gave him a tour of the house and the gardens. Hours later when the first excitement had calmed, Patrick handed me a small coin purse. "I really did earn it. I was a little short on the total needed to buy a ticket when Aadi found me. But I would like you to know I did try to find my own way here."

I couldn't hurt his pride. I accepted the payment and later had Aadi take it to be invested, though I did not mention this to Patrick not wishing to insult him. It was the best way I could think to help give Patrick a financial start for his future.

In a rush, I then explained everything to him about my uncle, the clues, the key, and the requirements of the will.

He studied the key for a moment before remarking, "Your uncle was rather complicated.

Pretty quick of you to get this far along."

I confess I felt a great sense of joy having my efforts admired, but quickly sobered. "Still, we only have a few months left to solve this or we lose the house, the money, and everything."

CHAPTER 6

Change of Pace

A week later, I invited the colonel over for tea. It was to introduce him to Patrick, and I was delighted when they became instant companions. Patrick made friends easily. Even the monkey, who seemed to be a part of the house now, followed him everywhere, often perching on his shoulder and eating bits of fruit from his hand.

After a time, the colonel remarked casually, "I'm traveling north tomorrow. Mr. Gray is coming as well. Been trouble at a few small villages and we're going help."

"What kind of trouble?" I asked curiously.

"There's two tigers that have taken to eating man." I choked on my coffee. I had heard of some tigers going rogue and becoming man-killers, but it was one thing to read about it in England and quite another to hear it firsthand in the jungle.

The colonel handed the ever-present monkey a mango and stated, "I only hunt animals if it's necessary. I've hunted four tigers, one elephant, and one leopard. All had killed, mostly children. If they are a menace, I hunt them to protect people. These tigers have killed seven people between them. The villagers have no way to defend themselves. I'm starting up first thing, at dawn. Would both of you like to join me?"

Patrick's yes was eager, and mine was hesitant. But we were going. The morning sun found us out on our way with home far behind and tigers too near ahead. I soon found myself thoroughly happy, sleeping deep in the jungle with a troop of native peoples who knew many fabulous tales of India, and tigers, and heroes. And though some of the stories made me wish for my safe room and warm bed, still that element of adventure was thrilling.

When at last we reached the first village, we made camp among them. The colonel had visited here before and was on friendly terms with this village. We soon had the story. Two young tigers, thought to be from the same mother, had been raiding the village herds. Then two months before our journey, a British hunting party had come through and maimed one of the animals. Being injured, she had taken to easier prey;

the village girls who went down to the river for water every morning. It made me quite glad that my jungle home had its own water well secure within the gates. At least Ida would never have a tiger stalk her while she brought in the water pails.

Mr. Gray was very grim when the colonel related this story to us, "People ought to be better shots, waste of time to injure a creature and leave it suffering enough to recourse to man-killer."

The lawyer's ideology surprised me, but I could see how the colonel and he had been able to see past their differences of India and respect the honorable huntsman in each other.

Of course, Mr. Gray still did not care for my company, nor did I care for his and we had done quite well at avoiding each other on this journey. He had taught Patrick the rudiments of gun care and steady aim, Patrick having never held, much less fired, a weapon before.

For two weeks we tracked the tiger's territory, baiting them only to be outwitted time after time. I am saddened to recall that during these days the tigers killed again, this time a young man who had been tending to his herds. The colonel and Mr. Gray decided to split our forces.

The beaters (who went through the brush clanging drums causing such a noisy stir that animals traveled away from the sound and toward the waiting guns of the hunters) came down a hill several miles away while I, Mr. Gray, and the colonel staked out points in a semi-circle distance from each other. The main outfitter, Sulek, who had led the expedition stayed with me. I was relieved to have another pair of eyes with me, though he did not bear a gun, as injuring even a dangerous animal was forbidden by his religion.

Many hours went by, a fly buzzed my face and I swatted at it. My mind trailed off a few times to other matters, but I kept my eyes and ears attentive to the attention at hand. A startling gunshot broke the monotony. It was probably a half-mile off. That would be the colonel's gun. Another shot followed, then silence. For away in the blue sky, buzzards began circling.

"One at least is dead," Sulek remarked.

My skin felt prickly and my hands were sweating. Where was the other tiger? Was it dead too or watching us from the tall grass? I glanced behind me at the large pool of water which reflected my scared face. At least if the tiger got behind us, we would hear the water splash. A few hundred yards away, I could make out Mr. Gray and Patrick, who had chosen two tall trees as their waiting place. The tiger's path should cross by them. I was merely the backdoor guard which was the safest place to be.

A long time passed, only the buzzards and the clouds were moving. Suddenly I heard Sulek inhale sharply and I followed his point to a place in the grass. The tall grass was moving opposite to the windblown field.

I raised my gun and waited, very shakily. Then I saw it. The long body, sleek hide, and twitching tail of a young Bengal Tiger. It was a second later when I realized she was actually coming toward me. Another second and her eyes locked onto mine.

"Fire, Sahib!" Sulek hissed. I squeezed the trigger. And missed. The tiger charged, I pulled up to fire again, but my gun jammed, I yelled, though I don't know what I said.

I heard a shot, once, twice; someone shouted. The beast's great paws engulfed me and we fell back into the pool.

The heavy body lay on top of me twitching. I could not move, and I could not breathe. The shallow pool was deeper than I had thought, and the weight of the tiger pressed me into the soft sandy floor. The water turned red, and I saw shadows above me, and a roaring was in my ears. I was drowning.

There were splashes, the tiger was dragged off, and I was pulled up gasping for breath and feeling very foolish. Patrick was shaking me asking if I was alive and the colonel came running up asking me if anything was broken. I had some claw marks, but not too deep as the creature had died before she could inflict serious damage. I was also terribly bruised, but no broken bones as the soft sand had given way enough to keep the tiger from crushing me.

Mr. Gray examined my gun and told me not to worry. I had done well on my first hunt. I soon found out that it was Mr. Gray who saved my life. Having realized the tiger had managed to go around our trap, he soon spotted her movement in the tall grass. And the bullets were so close that it made only one bullet hole. The colonel had dispatched of the other tiger and there would be a celebration in the villages that night. Amidst all this, Patrick burst into a laugh.

"Oh, James, do you know what you said when the tiger leaped at you?" I was chagrined to say I did not know.

"You said 'yard by yard!'"

I even laughed at this as I realized how much even in turmoil my mind subconsciously thought on my puzzling inheritance.

The next morning, we packed and headed home. It had been refreshing to step away and see the world a bit, but now I was very eager to return home. I smiled when I realized that Jokhim Manor was home, and I belonged there.

With the tiger hunt behind me, and my life preserved by Mr. Gray, I felt ashamed of my poor opinion of him. He was very British, but he seemed to be a man of some principle and despite his abrasive personality we managed to live on friendly terms during our travel afterwards.

Change of Pace

The night before we arrived home, I heard Patrick talking aloud to himself in the dark. I crept over by him and realized the monkey, *our* monkey, had come from home to find us. I slipped quietly back to my blanket and watched Patrick and his pet enjoying the moon rising far above the jungle. I knew that we all belonged together, and I grit my teeth with determination. I had to solve this riddle!

CHAPTER 7

Patrick's Help

After arriving home, both the colonel and Mr. Gray only stayed long enough for tea; they too were eager to return to their homes.

Patrick was a natural-born storyteller and had all the servants laughing for many days over different moments of our journey. He relished telling how the tiger had tackled me, but he was gracious too, and said my first shot missing its mark was probably the weapon's fault. I laughed and shook my head and acknowledged that my shot was a poor one.

Lipika shrieked in dismay on hearing of my startling encounter, but I quickly assured her that the tiger had been quite dead before it could have really harmed me, which then brought on the part in the tale about my torn shirt and cuts on my shoulder and Lipika shrieked again.

Aadi then told me that his mother was an exceptional seamstress and could fix my shirt or make a new one.

"I can buy you fabric by the bolt or by the yard," he ended.

I stared at him. Of course, I was so ignorant, yard by yard; two yards of fabric sown together. I grabbed Patrick's arm and called for Aadi to follow. We raced upstairs to my uncle's bedchambers and unlocked the wardrobe. I pulled out the shawl that belonged to my aunt; the same one the monkey had dragged to the tree that day.

We laid it out on the floor, the lace had torn in several places, and I smoothed it to lay flat as well as I could. For a moment we stared at it, and I thought worriedly that I was on the wrong trail. Suddenly, Patrick let out a cry of discovery.

"It's a map, the lace! It's a map of the gardens!" He pointed to the box-shaped rosettes on the hem, "the walls," a few embroidered sections, "the walkways," and a circle in the middle or "the well." We went outside with our map, and it did indeed match the layout of the grounds.

"I suppose the center is the key," Aadi remarked, and we all looked toward the well. Patrick winked and undressed to his waist. "Lower me down," he ordered. I told him it wasn't safe, but he defended the action, "I owe you something, James."

Grabbing the rope, he demanded to be lowered down. Aadi and I carefully lowered him until a splash told us he was at the water level. Without hesitation, Patrick dunked beneath the water. I bit my lip, what if he hit his head and drowned? What if? But before any more dreadful thoughts could come, he resurfaced holding a small metal box. We hauled him up and soon he stood dripping and triumphant.

The box was sealed in wax, even covering the keyhole.

"To keep the contents dry," remarked Aadi. We trooped inside and Aadi used a candle flame to melt the wax. With nervous hands, I used the key found in the chandelier and was pleased to hear a click. The box was unlocked.

I raised the lid and we all peeked in. The only thing inside was a multipage letter. Our disappointment was acute. I read the heading written in my uncle's broad, large-lettered writing that had also marked the margins of the library books.

"*Dear Richard* (that was my father), *I'm relieved to know you are reading this letter. I've written you numerous times and mother as well. But as I've never had a response from either of you, I concluded that all of you are still angered that I left. I did find adventure and riches . . . and love. I had a charming wife, Richard; I regret you will never meet her as she has preceded me to eternity.*

I am glad you finally came to see my home here, but as you are reading this letter, it means I am dead as well. It does take some of the satisfaction away.

I must relate a tale to you, it's too impossible to be false and I trust you will be wiser than I on how to handle it. A few years ago, I and two friends, Henry and Clement, all put our money together and bought a mine in the Kush mountains. For two years, it was grand, we had an entire crew, our fortunes doubled, aye even tripled. We had struck a rich deposit of lapis lazuli, and our future looked bright. The end of the second year, production was abruptly halted one morning. The workmen ran out of the mine in panic and would not enter again for any price.

Of course, I was always brash and, grabbing lanterns, I led Henry and Clement into the shaft. Deep in the rock, we found a massive door, ornately carved with a lion holding a sword and above it words in a language I did not know.

The door would not budge, and we exited to come back with an axe and hammer. As we reentered the mine, our crewmen chief stood in the doorway screaming for us to abandon the quest shouting, "It is cursed, cursed I tell you!"

Back at the door, we pounded away fruitlessly finally resorting to a pickax.

For a day and a half, we chopped through that door. When at last we had enough space for us to crawl through, we entered

Patrick's Help

one by one. I cannot tell you what the moment was like. The room glittered in the lantern's light, as if stars dwelled here. We had discovered a vast treasure by complete accident. Jewels, gold, elaborate figurines surpassing description lay about with chests and leather bags overflowing with their bounty.

We each picked a piece from the treasure and took it outside for examination. Once outside, we gabbled excitedly like children on Christmas Eve. I had chosen a sword encased in glorious scabbard with a jeweled hilt. It had been lying on a table of gold in the center of the treasure. A parchment paper was wrapped about the base of the scabbard. I unrolled it to find a written narrative in the same language as the engraving on the door.

After much begging, yelling, and nigh unto threatening we could not convince the crew to stay and they all abandoned camp. The chief made only this parting remark to me, "The door read 'whoso disturbs this chamber shall reap curses and sorrow.'" I scoffed and my friend and I determined to continue excavating the treasure. The next morning, Clement entered ahead of us to light torches and without warning the mine collapsed. We eventually dug out his body, still near the entrance, and buried him.

Disheartened we began our journey back to Calcutta. I still had that sword with me, but Edward was sick of treasure and had buried his piece with Clement. A week later, deep in the jungle, Edward was killed by the marsh crocodiles that inhabit those *regions. I buried him and continued my journey. Now I was sick in mind and body and disoriented with malaria.*

I began to be hounded by guilt and still I kept claim to that sword. A band of marauders caught sight of me and came charging, firing rifles. One bullet struck me in the shoulder. Crazed with fever, I drew the sword from its sheath and ran at them screaming. They saw the weapon and (though I can hardly say why I thought this) they seemed to recognize it and ran from me as if I had been an evil omen.

At last, I reached the edges of Kasauli and found myself going through the ruined palace. I hid the sword there and entered the town. Here I met Colonel Edward Baker, we became fast friends. A short time later I purchased the ruins and there set up my estate. I had met a beautiful woman who deserved a beautiful home. And my sword needed to be guarded.

Let me halt for a moment and tell you about her. On an excursion to a large village, I met Kashvi. She was the seventeenth child of a maharaja's third wife. Her father did not even know her name, but there she was at the festival, beautiful and sad. I obtained by many payments her dowry and she became my wife. But this time that dreaded sword did seem cursed to me, and I kept it hidden, telling no one of its existence. Two strange men soon began to appear, like shadows they followed me on hunts and town excursions.

These men knew I had some secret treasure, and they once broke into the house, only fleeing because my pet dog chased them away. One day in town I casually told my lawyer that I kept a certain piece in a chair cushion. One of the men must have heard, for two chairs were stolen from my study.

To rush my narrative, Kashvi died, and my malaria returned. I knew I had but a short time left to forever hide that cursed blade. You remember how I built my contraptions? I have spent a year creating this puzzle so that only someone who knows me well can solve it. I had thought to destroy the sword, but I confess I am terrified of it so it is safely hidden, and you can decide what is to be done with it.

But be warned, I have, after much study, translated the document that came wrapped on the sheath. I have left my copy of it with the weapon. When you find it, you will understand my fears.

Look for my mark, and you will behold it. May this house bring you what has been missing for me.

Your loving brother, Robert."

I finished reading and looked at Patrick and Aadi. Both were silent for a moment. Aadi was the first to speak.

"This explains the missing and moved furniture. Since your uncle died, it has continued. They must know the house well, for no candles are ever noticed, they can go about in the dark."

Patrick looked a bit grim, then his eyes sparkled.

"But we know the chair remark is a false lead. All we need is to find the 'mark' your uncle left for us."

I, of course, had not the slightest clue what his mark was or what exactly had been meant by his building "contraptions." But we knew our time was getting shorter every day. We had to work fast.

CHAPTER 8

Deeper Thinking

The next morning, the colonel came by. He was leaving for another medical round in the jungle and had stopped to say farewell.

I regretted he would be gone for two months and felt anxious about our circle of trustees shrinking.

"Did my uncle mention making contraptions?" I asked completely out of the blue.

The colonel chuckled as he swung back into Napoleon's saddle. "Yes, he liked to make little mechanisms. He made me a lock for my medical cabinet. It doesn't require a key or a combination. You merely have to know the secret to swiveling the bolt open. Clever piece of work." He saluted to us all and cantered out of the gate.

The next day had an interesting reprieve to losing friends and solving riddles.

At breakfast, Patrick asked me about the temple ruins he had seen on a distant hill as he had traveled on his journey to live with me. He said it couldn't be more than ten miles from my house. I nodded and said I had noticed them but hadn't considered it further. Patrick was shocked.

"James, really, you have a poor sense of adventure." I laughed heartily and agreed as I drank my coffee. But that was not the end of it.

As Ida poured my second coffee of the morning (I had not only grown accustomed to the drink, but I also thoroughly liked it now), Patrick asked her about the temple ruins. She was familiar with them and said she had visited more than once.

"It is magic there," she whispered, her words haunting me with the adventure in them. I made up my mind.

"Patrick, let's go see it."

Of course, it couldn't be done that very minute. We first procured a villager that had elephants and started off the next morning. Ida rode on an elephant with me as I had no idea what I was doing, and Patrick who had a knack for animals rode on another. Those ten miles, traveling atop an elephant in a jungle were wonderful. The sunlight streaming through the greenery, flowers hanging about on vines. I plucked one

Deeper Thinking

and gave it to Ida. The monkey ran above us in the trees, occasionally dropping down to ride with Patrick.

When we neared the ruins, Ida slowed her elephant and Patrick did the same. And suddenly, stones and towers seem to emerge from the jungle, with doors and stairs leading about and beckoning to be explored. We dismounted and indulged in every childlike whim we liked. We went about our exploration leaving no corner unseen. It was beautiful, eerie, and like Ida had said, it was magic. Finally tired out, we sat down at the top of a stair ornate with carvings peeking through the moss. Lipika had packed us food and we felt like great explorers eating our well-earned dinner with the ruins below us.

Our conversation turned to our inheritance puzzle, and we were all quite animated talking about what we would do if we found ourselves suddenly rich. Even Ida joined in, her eyes sparkling as she and Patrick discussed the things they would do and places they would go. And I wanted them to have all of that. Every opportunity and every dream. But that only happened if I succeeded. My face must have shown my worry for I found both of them staring at me. Patrick smiled, "Don't worry, James, you're going to figure it out. And we're here to help any way we can."

Ida smiled and nodded too, and I laughed. "Yes, we will solve the riddle." I hoped my tone sounded more confident than I felt. It was very late in the afternoon when we rode back home through the jungle. The jungle sounds truly enchanted me now, the setting sun turning the green world red and orange. And then I saw my home nestled in the glowing dusk ahead. I loved it here.

That night as I lay in bed watching the monkey balance on the window ledge, I had the oddest thought that he was disappointed in how slow my brain was working. I laughed to myself. "I agree," I muttered before falling asleep and not thinking again until waking at the dawn.

I had counted out the weeks left, already I had called Jokhim House home for thirty weeks. More than half the time allotted to trying to solve this riddle. Time passed too quickly and very pleasantly during this time; I had written my grandmother every week but had not heard from England. That changed today, for as the colonel left, Aadi returned from the village bearing two letters.

I eagerly read through them and was overcome with grief. Tennyson had written the letters, one to tell that my grandmother had died, some of her last words being, "I'm proud of James. I should have told him so." I confess I was weeping by the time I started the second letter.

The house was sold to pay off the remaining debts, and Tennyson was leaving for Wales to work at his sister and brother-in-law's farm.

"I cannot work for anyone else; I do not wish to have any other service. Your grandmother, and the Harris family was the only home I ever tended, and I cannot bear to have another in its place. Farewell, I wish you the best in India. There is nothing for you to return to England for."

I went to my room and cried until I could no longer shed tears. I had lost my father, mother, grandmother, uncle, and even my childhood home in my fourteen years of life. And at the moment it felt unbearable.

Lipika slipped in and, though it is generally considered against the rules of servants, she wrapped her arms around me in silent comfort. Patrick and his monkey brought me dinner, and I thanked them humbly.

That night wore by slowly and for the first time, I watched a moon complete its nightly march through the sky. As the sun came up, I sat in the window watching the first rays brush the jungle alive with color. Though by now I had learned that the jungle never really sleeps.

My tired mind thought dully on the riddle and I ached to solve it, to keep a home for Patrick, myself, Aadi, Ida, Lapaki, Yatin, and even that silly monkey. I so desperately wanted all of us to be able to stay a family. I had to find the missing piece, the sword, and Mr. Gray had to verify me as the owner for this life to continue.

Patrick tiptoed in and asked quietly, "Are you alright?"

I gave him a weary smile. "Of course, thank you for everything, Patrick."

He gave me a sheepish grin and sat down beside me as we watched the jungle morning.

We worked tirelessly as a team over the next few days, searching the house thoroughly. I also purchased two Bakharwal dogs, a famed Himalayan guard dog breed. After the dogs arrived, we had no more break-ins, and the furniture was left in peace.

Eight more weeks went by and I was beginning to feel frantic. Patrick tried hard to make me laugh as often as he could, which was daily. That chance meeting in Calcutta had won me a friend that was true as any hero in the books I had so loved to read.

Aadi and Ida often helped in the search, but despite our best efforts, we found no leads. It was late one evening and Patrick was sitting on the floor, his legs crossed, as he worked through an encyclopedia. Aadi and I had given him hardly any rest on his education, and I am proud to boast that he was becoming a man of learning. He was a naturally gifted linguist and learned rapidly.

Suddenly he looked up, "James! What if his mark is not a symbol or initials or any of the things we have searched for."

"What would it be then?"

"Perhaps it is just what he said, 'a mark!'"

For several minutes we thought deeply, every thought that came we soon discarded as impractical. As we sat deep in reverie, I heard the dogs give a sharp bark. Aadi soon entered to announce Mr. Gray. It was raining softly outside and Mr. Gray was wet and chilled. He quickly ordered Aadi to bring coffee and stoked the fire. I had the fire going for the draft, for the rain had brought down the mountain air. Once Mr. Gray was feeling more comfortable, he began in his most business manner.

"Mr. Harris, you have twenty weeks left until the tenure is up. Are you going to complete this 'game' by then?"

I was irked by his manner, but of course, one cannot be terse with the man who has saved your life.

"I think we shall be able to sign as the owners within the remaining weeks."

He looked doubtful but shrugged and brought out a paper.

"This is your copy of the deed if you can call anything a proper deed in India. Of course, it is not *authorized* as of yet.

You may read over it and understand the entire fortune and the estate entailings." He handed it over. "I hope to conclude this business soon. And please have Aadi restrain the dogs so I may depart without a mauling."

In response, Patrick gave a shrill whistle and both dogs trooped in shaking wet fur. Mr. Gray raised his eyebrows, finished his coffee, and left with a respectful bow. Clearly, Patrick's ease of control over the dogs had left a favorable impression on the lawyer.

I read through the document full of ambiguous words and jargon. It was ponderous reading, to say the least.

"You could imagine they could make the point more obvious," I remarked dryly putting the paper down. The monsoon season in India had clearly dulled my senses.

Suddenly, I smacked my forehead and jumped out of the chair.

"Patrick, Aadi!" I shouted. Both started sharply and stared at me, this behavior was extremely out of the ordinary for myself. I clasped my hands behind my back and paced the floor. "It's obvious, so obvious in fact that I feel the fool for taking so long to see it. The clues all started with my uncle's tombstone, and they all end with my aunt's. Link by link, the key on the chandelier chain; yard by yard, my aunt's shawl which was a map to the well where we found the letter. The last clue tells us to find his 'mark'! My aunt's gravestone reads, 'This place MARKS no grave, only memory!'"

I quite yelled this last part so that the monkey, who hung on the rafters gave a screech. I looked up at him and laughed, "And you monkey pet seemed to know all along, you pulled the shawl out and led me to the gravesite."

Patrick leaped up and grabbed my arm as we galloped about the room in ecstasy. "James, you're a genius!" he sang, and Aadi smiled admirably at me though he retained his dignity.

CHAPTER 9

Final Steps

We had a tiresome wait of two more weeks before monsoon season completed the long ritual visit. At last, Patrick and I were headed down the path. Nearly two months of rain had grown the jungle so much that we had to cut our way through, once or twice unsure of where the graveyard was. At last, we found it again, and cleaned the stones to read the words.

The words were all capitalized and for a moment I hesitated. I looked at Patrick who grinned, "Come along, James. You will know what to do."

I looked back and studied the works. Running my finger along M, A, R, and K. I noticed the triangle in the "A" seemed to protrude out slightly. I thought of the colonel's lock my uncle had made. "You just need to know the secret of swiveling the bolt open," I repeated to myself.

One more moment of thought and I pushed the blank space in the A. It clicked in, there was a grinding and whirring sound. The gravestone gave a shudder then and with much groaning shifted back to reveal a small shaft with stairs leading down. A dark stale air and slight draft rustled out of the space and the hair raised on my neck.

We looked at each other. "My mother's lineage says not to trespass on a gravesite. My British side says go in," Patrick remarked as he tore a strip off his shirt and proceeded to make a torch. Once the flame was burning, we stepped down into the hold with much trepidation.

The stairway was carved from solid stone and led to a large room. An iron wheel which controlled the door was to our left and a large gold table was on the far side. The walls had specks of glitter and upon examination proved to be covered from floor to ceiling with tiles of pure lapis lazuli. The floor was laid in white marble and had large emeralds set in it shaped to spell the name Kashvi.

We very reverently approached the table, made from solid gold with a jewel-covered mask of a tiger hanging on the wall behind it. There on the table lay the sword, its hilt so covered in diamonds that I couldn't even see the gold beneath it. A parchment was folded beside it, and I opened to see a narrative carefully written in an ancient language. Beneath it was folded the translation.

I read the translation aloud.

"I, Adel Shah, write these words in my own hand. I, myself confess to aiding in secrecy in the murder of Nader Shah, my previous lord and uncle. I and those, whose names I will not reveal, killed the world's most feared tyrant. The great temples of skulls stand testimony to his cruelty and the land did weep with relief at his passing. I have become the king in his stead and my hand has been heavy, and I fear to die young for the title I have taken.

The night of the assassination we of the conspiracy hid the sword of Nader, for no such weapon of atrocities should be left to continue its evil work. I supplied from the vast reserves left by Nader much gold and diamonds and commanded a replica sword and sheath created. I ordered the bladesmith to remain silent of this deed, by oath that if broken would curse his family for a thousand generations as well as promising a torturous death for the bladesmith.

I then presented this copy of the sword publicly, proclaiming that by the death of the former Shah I retained the power of the All-Conquering Sword. Only I and the conspirators knew that it was not the same blade.

I have had to flee to Tehran, my brother leads a more powerful army against me. The darkness swiftly approaches and already I have prepared the place to be the tomb for the weapon. My trusted advisor has taken the sword to hide it there forever. A great carved door bars the entry and a hundred curses placed upon the head of the one who should dare to open it. I have ordered much treasure to be hidden with it to appease the spirit in the mountain. May it be forgiving and hold within its darkness this evil weapon and never let it be released into the hand of man again.

As I write my eyes grow dim and I see the face of Nader, cruel and evil, glaring at me from beyond the grave. But I would not destroy the sword so that in the afterlife he could not possess it again. So long as it remains upon earth whole, its power will not embody again the form of Nader. To this end, I have won and do not fear his glaring eye.

To whomever may be fool enough to enter the sword's lost lair, and to read my words, may you never have peace until you lay this sword to a crypt again, so that the evil will not begin anew.

I have written it and it shall be.

Adel Shah, King of this land."

Our eyes were frightened as we looked at each other and Patrick backed away from the table.

"I have heard the dreadful tales from the horrors that the ruler Nader Shah did in Delhi.

Some will not even speak his name for fear the evil of his spirit may return."

I looked around the room. "This place was built in guilt; I think my uncle believed possession of this sword brought about the death of his wife and his friends. He put much wealth into this place as a proper tomb to 'appease' the sword."

Patrick nodded, "So what shall we do?"

"Leave it here and destroy all the clues my uncle left. It is wisest to not touch that which is so evil."

"Glad that I am not so squeamish," a familiar voice said coolly. We jumped, and grabbing each other's arms, we turned around.

There stood the lawyer, Mr. Gray, and behind him two men I did not know.

CHAPTER 10

From Beginning to End

"I knew your uncle had something from the Nader Shah treasure, but I never imagined it could be something so marvelous. The man the world feared only a century ago, the Sword of Persia. And here lies his very sword!"

"You have no right to take it!" Patrick snapped, oh I admired his fearless tone, my own mouth was dry, and I felt nauseated.

"I have more right to it than a street urchin and a wealthy brat," he replied with an edge to his voice.

"My brother Clement died for your uncle's foolishness. All the wealth he had earned in the mine and the loss of his life, this at least will ease the pain." He strolled across the room and snatched it up. His eyes were bright as he unsheathed it and the blade seemed to gleam red in the torchlight.

"For years I searched until I found where the mine had been. There was a rude grave with Clement Gray on it. That's all, nothing else, just a lonely place in a barren land. Your uncle could have at least got him a proper tombstone. So I searched more and found your uncle alive, the only one left of the three. I became his friend and by talks and spies," motioning to the two men, "I learned that he does indeed have a treasure hidden. No matter how I try, I cannot conduct a proper search nor retrieve any information from him. But then he dies, and I finally have time to truly look for it. For months I searched for the 'missing piece.' I found nothing. I finally determined that his brother, the heir, perhaps he would lead me to it. But he was already dead. My frustration was overwhelming till I learned that YOU were the next heir in line. I could only hope that a boy should know his uncle well enough to find it. Imagine my chagrin to find that you had never met him! And yet here we are, and you did in a few months what I could not do in years. These two men are the detectives that formally worked for your grandmother. Your Aunt Kashvi paid them off to never find your uncle. She was a jealous person and loved Robert passionately and selfishly. So Indian indeed. And now these gentlemen work for me."

"Well, that's not passionate or selfish for you?" Patrick sneered. One of the henchmen drew a revolver, "Shut it!" He loomed toward us.

Mr. Gray twirled the sword expertly. "But this piece, this is greater than I could have hoped! It is something to make up for poor Clement." His voice was angry and empty.

"It won't help!" I was shocked that I was speaking. "Patrick and I have lost our families.

But a trinket won't make them come back."

He pointed that sword at me, "You are certainly a unique fellow, almost worthy of swordplay, but your tender years will spare you."

At that moment, Patrick dove at the man with the gun and I attempted to assist. Somehow the gun went off aimed at the mechanical wheel that opened the door. There was the ear-shattering rattle of breaking chains, the wheel rolled back to its original place, the door above slammed closed.

For a moment we all froze staring at each other in horror. Then there was shouting, and Mr. Gray pointed his blade uncomfortably close to my throat. "Alright, you're the clever one, open it!" he thundered.

I looked over the mechanism, but it could only be reworked with tools, and the broken chain would no longer do its service.

I looked at Patrick overwhelmed and hopeless. We were entombed in this place with that dreadful sword.

"Perhaps you could find a secret door," Patrick joked weakly. But there were no more clues that I could think of to help. I sat still for a time thinking, everyone was staring at me expectantly. Finally, one thing came to me as interesting, and odd.

"There's a draft down here. The air must come from somewhere."

Everyone scrambled to look for cracks in the wall or ceiling. But I didn't. I stared at the gold table and the tiger mask. It came to my mind strange that he should have chosen to place a mask in this tomb. I knew from my reading that the tiger represented courage and strength. Why put that symbolism down here? I walked over and climbed atop the table to reach the mask. I ran my hands along the edges, but it was firmly attached. The eyes had been set with rubies and the nose inset with diamonds. The stripes were tempered gold and the mouth outlined in black pearls. It was exquisite, a work of art and untold richness. Had my uncle left this as a sign to be brave and that was all, or was there more? My uncle seemed to always mean more than he said. I thought until my head hurt, going through all the things he had written, every clue he left, and every answer that we had found. I thought of the books in my uncle's library. Ranging from *Romeo and Juliet* to the *Odyssey*.

I ran my finger along the tiger mask's open mouth and shivered as I remembered my close encounter with a live one.

It was hard to comprehend that only weeks before Mr. Gray had saved my life and now, he threatened it. I had read about gold sickness, where the search for treasure can drive men to madness.

I touched an ivory fang on the mask and noticed how every tooth in the tiger's mouth was solid ivory. I stopped. Was my imagination or were there letters etched into some of the teeth? I looked closer. I was sure now, there were thirty teeth and, on some, letters irregularly carved, and not in alphabetical order. The mask was life-sized. It was a bit eerie to reach into the gaping mouth. Patrick suddenly was at my elbows.

"You found something," he stated, his eyes twinkling with the new clue to unwind.

The three men crowded close behind us, anxious to be out of the hole, but suspicious of me too. No one spoke. I studied the letters and tried to unscramble what words it might be meant to spell. C, A, E, E, P; what clue had he left that I had missed?

The key, the shawl, the letter, the sword, and now a word. My mind raced and I felt a little sick. My father who had known my uncle would have understood this last surprise with the "missing piece" in a hidden room.

"No!" I exclaimed aloud and everyone jumped a little.

"I've had it all wrong. The sword is not the missing piece, he knew where that was all the time. The sword was never missing. It's a play on words, his life was sad, almost tragic, he was missing 'PEACE!'"

I spelled it out, pushing each marked tooth in the correct order. There was a grinding and loud crack. The mask shifted away from me as the entire wall swung open to reveal a long dark tunnel. For a moment no one moved, then Mr. Gray climbed over the table and headed up the tunnel, calling back, "Bring them."

Patrick and I were grabbed by the shirt collar and nearly dragged along. We walked for some distance with the torchlight throwing weird shadows on the floor. Once a tarantula scurried away from us, but otherwise, it was a lonely place. Then quite unexpectedly, the tunnel made a dead end. Stair rungs stretched to the roof and a large lever was on the wall at the top accompanied by another wheel and chain.

"No surprises here. The lever opens a trap door," Mr. Gray remarked as he ordered one of the former detectives to climb up and open the door.

The mechanism was trigged, and a door raised up letting in light and fresh air. We all climbed out blinking. Far behind us, I heard a groan and the ground shuddered as a loud banging sound echoed in the tunnel.

"The wall with the mask must have slammed shut," I remarked to Patrick. So that room was sealed within itself once again. I was not sorry to know it.

Mr. Gray suddenly gave a little laugh, and I reached the top of the ladder to discover that the trap door led to the study in Jokhim House. The door was underneath the heavy desk which raised up by a lever to reveal the tunnel beneath.

If the situation had been less terrible, I would have laughed as well. The last laugh really belonged to my uncle. So clever to put a secret in plain view and leave an escape route.

"Now I truly don't wish to kill you, so you will bid me adieu and I will take my find and leave this accursed country," Mr. Gray said putting the sword into its elaborate sheath. "No one need know about this event. I daresay the jewels can be released from this sword and will serve to keep me rich for life." He examined the weapon. "Though it does seem a shame to destroy it so."

"Bad things have happened with that sword, and you know too well that someone will try to take it from you just like you have taken it. Hidden treasure gives its owner no rest." My voice was firm, but I daresay it squeaked some.

"My, you are the philosopher," he remarked dryly. He turned to leave the room. But in the doorway stood Aadi, with a curious whiplike weapon in his hand.

"You will not leave this house without the Malika's permission. I was in the hallway as the desk opened. I know you have robbed and threatened my Malika, and as his headman, I will defend him."

"So Indian of you," Mr. Gray drawled unsheathing the sword. His men pulled out their pistols, but Mr. Gray waved them back.

"No, I'm quite thrilled to see how bloodthirsty this legendary sword really is. Do not interfere. I've wanted to teach this servant brat a lesson for a long time."

In answer, Aadi flipped his wrist and the whip blade smashed against the floor with a deafening clang. The whole group of us moved out into the hallway for more space.

Patrick gave a startling whistle, and everyone turned about when two massive bounds of fur came galloping down the hall toward us. The men raised their weapons, but Patrick bit one of the men's arms and I kicked my captor in the knee. Then the dogs were there. Loud clangs told me that two men, experts in their craft, were beginning a duel.

Mr. Gray was exceptional in the art of the curved blade, but Aadi's weapon had greater reach, and he was as comfortable swinging that terrifying weapon about his body as a painter is in sliding his brush over a canvas. Mr. Gray could not get close enough to attack his opponent.

It was over soon. The dogs had severely injured the two thieves and Mr. Gray's right arm was cut so deeply it was nearly dis-attached. The dreadful sword lay on the ground with its newest master's own blood dripping onto it. I was surprised to Lipika, Ida, and Yatin staring open-mouthed. No one spoke and there really wasn't anything to say.

I was thankful that the colonel had returned the day before and he was soon brought to tend to the serious wounds of our assailants.

"And what are we to do with them?" Patrick asked me as I cleaned that horrible blade which had caused so much grief. "I suppose we could let them go," I said with a shrug. "To be honest, they're almost petty thieves. They stole furniture and attempted to take the sword. They did threaten us, but as they haven't succeeded, I don't see that real charges should be brought."

Patrick eyed me, "You really are so very strange, my friend." We both laughed, but I did as I said and let them go.

Epilogue

Mr. Gray was taken by the colonel, after his wounds healed, to Calcutta. He was almost a broken man now, having lost the sword and his supposed purpose of avenging his brother. I gave the colonel a great deal of money to see that Mr. Gray could return to England and set up as a lawyer. I knew though it would be some time before the man would be well and I made sure to give enough funds to tend to him for many years to come.

The two henchmen were terrified of the dogs and of Aadi and swore an oath never to return to India, which to my knowledge they never did. Aadi also began teaching me the art of *Kalaripayattu* fighting and the use of the *urumi* whip sword which I might add I mastered fairly well in time. The "missing piece" was indeed "peace" as I soon confirmed to finish the last step to inheritance. Another lawyer was brought and was dull enough not to be interested in the details and merely completed his task. He oversaw my estate until I turned eighteen, but he let me do as I saw fit with no interference. It was a great day for me when I was at last of age to claim full power over all of my inheritance. I celebrated by purchasing a copy of *A Christmas Carol* for my library.

Patrick later went to Paris and studied at several universities and traveled abroad extensively before returning home to India a very educated and very wealthy man.

As for me, I renamed Jokhim House to *Shaanti ka ghar* or "House of Peace." And I had many peaceful decades in my Indian home. The sword I have hidden, and I left no clues. I truly agree with my uncle that it was an evil weapon and should not see the light of day again. I hid it far from the grave and from the house. I rest easy, now as an old man, knowing that I did the right duty. And don't bother searching. I can assure you that some things are not meant to be found.

Facts or Fiction?

The term "Raj" referred to a time of British rule in India. Most of the British people that occupied India during this time had no respect for the people. Only a small few embraced the culture and appreciated the people as represented by Colonel Edward Baker in this story. He is fictional, but his respect for the country of India is very real.

The tiger hunt was based on actual tiger hunts conducted by Jim Corbett. You can read about some of his adventures in his writings such as his book *Man-Eaters of Kumaon*.

Nader Shah was a ruler of ancient Persia, now called Iran. Sometimes referred to as "the Sword of Persia," he was a powerful military leader who invaded India in 1739 leaving with riches that included the famous Peacock Throne.

The church that James visited is Christ Church, built in Kasauli in 1853.

The *urumi* is a type of sword used in some forms of Indian martial arts such as *Kalaripayattu*.

The Bakharwal dog breed is an ancient working dog breed that excels at guarding and livestock protection.

The famous sword of Nader Shah is in Tehran, Iran. *Or is it perhaps a mere duplicate of the original?*

From the Author

It has been a delight to share this bit of historical fact mixed with some imaginative fiction. History is sometimes referred to as a dead subject because all of the subjects are "dead." But history is being made every moment and our memory of it fades a little more every day. Don't accept one person's opinion on past facts as final. Always search it out for yourself. There are many books, articles, and web pages that can be poured through to find the truth of the matter. Be the next explorer of the past.

History lives on in you. But only if we preserve it.

www.ingramcontent.com/pod-product-compliance
Lightning Source LLC
LaVergne TN
LVHW020415070526
838199LV00054B/3616